OLiVia's Secret Scribbles

My NEW ♡ Best Friend

Kane Miller

A DIVISION OF EDC PUBLISHING

For Mickey Dewar, the very best of friends,
forever and always—M.C.

For my parents Judy and Mal. Thank you for your
constant love and support. x—D.M.

First American Edition 2019
Kane Miller, A Division of EDC Publishing

Text copyright © Meredith Costain, 2018
Illustrations copyright © Danielle McDonald, 2018

First published by Scholastic Australia Pty Limited in 2018.
This edition published under license from Scholastic Australia Pty Limited.

For information contact:
Kane Miller, A Division of EDC Publishing
PO Box 470663
Tulsa, OK 74147-0663
www.kanemiller.com
www.edcpub.com
www.usbornebooksandmore.com

Library of Congress Control Number: 2018942395

Printed and bound in the United States of America

1 2 3 4 5 6 7 8 9 10

ISBN: 978-1-61067-839-1

OLIVIA'S
BIG BOOK of
PRIVATE
SECRETS
DO NOT OPEN!
GO AWAY!

(This means you, Max,
and mainly you, Ella!!!)

Moving-day Thursday

This is the very first page of my special, private secrets book! And guess where I am writing it?

In my super-amazing new bedroom!

My new room is upstairs.

In the attic!

I am the only person in my whole family who has a bedroom with stairs. Not even my big sister, Ella, does, and she usually gets any new stuff first. Like clothes. And scooters. And real bikes.

ELLA

Grown-up
BiKE

ME

Little-
KiD Bike

But not this time. ☺

Hey! Do you want to know a secret?

Ella has a special writing book too! She's always hiding it in different places around the house, but she can't trick me. I have super detective skills. ☺

Once I found it in the dirty clothes basket, under all the smelly socks. Pee-eww. I couldn't read it because it was locked.

But mine is going to be so much more exciting and better than hers anyway!

Before I could move into my new room, we had to clear out all the old stuff. Good thing it's school vacation!

Dad wanted to get rid of everything.

This can go.

NO WAY!

Dad

What do you need a broken clock for?

To make my time machine go!

Then we painted some planets and twinkly stars on the ceiling.

I can see the whole world from up here!
Look at what I can see right now.

Mr. Pappas hanging
out his washing. He
has really ginormous
undies!

Mrs. Freeman
scaring parrots away
from her pear tree
with a water pistol.

Clothesline

Ginormous
UNDIES!

MR. Pappas's
PLACE

MRS. Freeman's
PLACE

parrots

SUPER
Soaker

Pear
Tree

EMPTY HOUSE

EMPTY BackYard

OUR BackYard

ELLA

Dad

Max

BOB

My window

The empty backyard behind ours. The house is empty too because all the people who lived there moved out last week. ☹

Max and Ella having a picnic with Dad and Bob in OUR backyard.

HEY!

They were supposed to wait for me!

Got to go!

☺livia

Mystery Friday

Someone's been in my new bedroom!!!

They've been looking in my special experiment cupboard. And moving stuff around!

At first I thought it might be Donkey. But Donkey would never do that.

Donkey lives next door. He likes to sleep on the roof outside my window. Sometimes he even comes inside and sleeps on my bed!

DoNKey is a BiG GRUMPY PanTS.

He gets especially grumpy if you pat and cuddle him when he's trying to sleep.

Donkey is also very smart. I think he would make a good detective cat. I'm going to train him to find out who's been sneaking into my room. ☺

Olivia

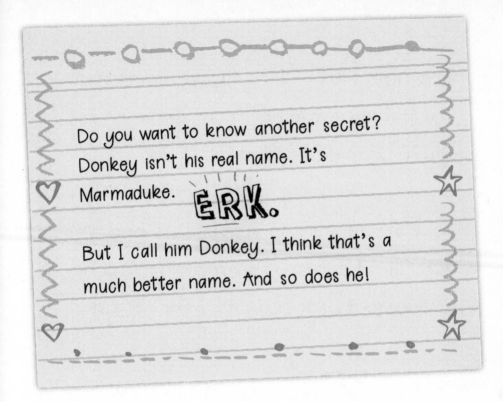

Do you want to know another secret? Donkey isn't his real name. It's Marmaduke. **ERK.**

But I call him Donkey. I think that's a much better name. And so does he!

Saturday Morning Sign Wars

I think __Ella__ is the someone who's been snooping in my room.

It's **not** fair! Ella is always telling me
I can't come into her room. Or touch her
stuff. Or even look at it!

So I accidentally on purpose let Bob
into Ella's bedroom this morning. And he
jumped onto her bed and woke her up!

And then he bounced around her room
and knocked some stuff off her shelf.
Oops! So then she made this sign and
stuck it on her door:

WARNING

NO DOGS

allowed in HERE at ANY time
(DAY OR NIGHT)
and especially EARLY in
the morning.
BY ORDER
of ELLA

So I made this sign and stuck it on my door!

So then Ella made another sign.

And so did I!

Then I remembered something about my little brother, Max. He is super messy. I don't want him coming into my room either.

MAX, the mess KING.

So I made
another sign.

That should make sure they **both** stay out!

☺livia

Saturday Afternoon

There are only two more sleeps till school goes back.

Usually, I  school.

Especially when we play games and make things. But going to school on Monday is going to be very sad because Lucy won't be there.

Lucy is my Best Friend in the Whole World. She ~~lives~~ used to live in the house on the other side of our back fence. (The one that is empty now.)

There's a big hole in the fence. We'd climb through it to visit each other.

We played games in our backyards

and swapped
special secrets

and had
sleepovers

and played funny tricks on Ella and her
BFF Zoe

and rode our
bikes in the park

and walked to school together.
Every day.

Last year, at school, our class made a whole family of plant pets out of grass seeds and old stockings.

Mine and Lucy's were the best. They had Super Hair!

Plant Pets

SUPER HAIR

Googly eyes

Stocking

Grass

Garden Pot

LUCY'S   MINE

But last week Lucy's family packed up all their beds and chairs and plates and games and toys and bikes into a ginormous truck. And then they moved away to a big city, far away.

So far away you can't even see it from my window. ☹

So now Lucy won't be there to walk to school with me. Or sit next to me in class. Or chase Harry and Nico around the playground.

Maybe I'll just stay home and play school with Donkey and Bob instead.

☹livia

Sunday Surprise!

We just came back from shopping with Dad. And guess what Donkey and I saw out my window?

A playhouse!

In the empty backyard behind our house!

Maybe new people moved in while we were out. New people **with kids!** Cool!

I'm going outside **right now** to find out!

A bit later

I'm back!

I just looked into their backyard through the hole in our fence. And this is what I saw.

They <u>do</u> have kids!

A little bit later after that

I just asked Mom if I could go
over to meet the new kids.

Mom,

Me: Mom? Can I go next door to meet the
new kids? And play in their playhouse?
Mom: Maybe another time, possum. It's
getting late. And you need to get your stuff
ready for school tomorrow.
Me: ☹☹☹
Mom: What's wrong? I
thought you loved school.
Me: Not anymore. Hey, can I have a
playhouse for my birthday?

Mom: But I thought you wanted a time machine?

Me: I'm already making my own. I just need a few more bits for it. Ple-e-e-ease can I have a playhouse? I'd let you come and play in it. 😉

Mom: Well, maybe. If you're good . . .

Me: Yay! I'm **always** good! 😊

And I am. Well, most of the time.

My playhouse is going to be bigger and better than the one next door. It is going to be the best playhouse ever!

Here are my plans for what it will look like.

Looks like I'll have to wait till tomorrow to meet the new kids. ☹

Hey! Maybe they'll be at my school! That would be awesome!

☺livia

Back-to-school Monday

I did go to school. And it was fun!

Our new teacher is called Mr. Platt. He doesn't have any plaits though. He's got a big bushy beard instead!

Mr. Platt likes juggling. And he tells really funny jokes and stories. Sometimes he even does both at the same time!

All the same kids are back in my class again. Except for one. ☹

But guess what? There is a new girl! Called Matilda!

Mr. Platt asked the class to say good morning to Matilda. Then he helped her find somewhere to sit. My table was already full with me, Ava and Daisy. And Hannah G.'s and Sage's tables were full too.
So Matilda sat next to Jamila and Ivy.

Jamila and Ivy sit at
the table in front of
mine. So the part of
Matilda that I could
see the most was

her back. And the back of her head.

Then Mr. Platt asked us to come up to the
front, one by one, to talk about the best
thing we did over vacation.

Nico talked about his camping trip. Jamila went to the movies three times. Ava got a bouncy new puppy called Benji. She said he is very licky. (Just like Bob.)

I told everyone about my new room at the top of our house. And how I can see everything from up there. Like the new playhouse on the other side of our back fence.

And Matilda stared at me the whole time I was talking.

Like this.

Spooky.

Then it was time for gym so we all went outside and played soccer. I scored two goals!

☺livia

Monday Afternoon Mystery

There are two little boys playing in the playhouse!

I think they might be twins. They look exactly the same! But I am not totally sure. So I am going to look through my binoculops to help me see better.

Oops! I meant **binoculars**. But I think **binoculops** is a much better name.

They *are* twins! They look the same size as Max. Maybe they can all be friends! And then I can play in their playhouse too. ☺

I wonder what their names are?

Fred AND Ed   Ed and TED
? Blake AND Jake
Jason and Mason ?
? Silly and Billy (hehe!)
?

I'm going to go over and ask them! Right
now!

Mystery solved!

I'm back!

I accidentally on purpose kicked a ball over our back fence. And then Bob and I crept through the hole to get it back. Right into their backyard!

The boys aren't called Silly and Billy. 😲 Their names are **Benny and Ollie.** And they loved Bob. He licked them all over! They don't have their own dog. But they do have a big sister! She was out shopping with their mom.

I was about to ask what her name was
when a big white bird flew over our heads.
So I looked up. And guess what I saw?

Someone up in my room!

So Bob and I rushed straight back home.

And guess what? Someone had been in my room! The door of my experiment cupboard was open! I'm 99% sure it was shut before.

I bet it was Ella. Or maybe Max.

Donkey was curled up on my bed. I asked him if he'd seen who came into my room, but he just yawned at me. I definitely need to start his special detective cat training soon!

☺livia

Monday night, after dinner

Here are my plans for an invention I am going to make. It will let me know for sure if people come into my room when I'm not here.

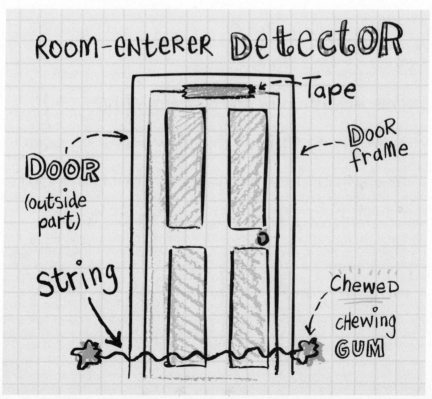

Room-enterer Detector

Tape

Door frame

DOOR (outside part)

String

Chewed chewing GUM

How it works:

If the tape is
broken and the
string is hanging
off sideways, it
means someone has
entered your room!

This invention is going to be *amazing!*
I am going to test it out when I go back
to visit our new neighbors tomorrow. But
first of all I need to find some tape.

Hehehe. I know where to get some.

Ella has LOTS of sticky tape in her big box of craft stuff. I'm going to sneak into her room and get some while she's helping Dad do the dishes. I'll be

right back. ☺

ELLA'S BIG BOX of CRAFT STUFF!

A bit later

Oops! That was close! She almost caught me! Good thing Bob is such a good actor. And guess what? It worked! ☺

The final thing I needed was some chewing gum. Luckily I had lots in my experiment cupboard. It was even already chewed!

Perfect!

☺livia

Charming Tuesday

I showed Ava and Daisy my special
friendship necklace at lunchtime today.

Ava

Daisy

Lucy has one too. Her mom gave them to
us, just before their family moved away.

The necklaces have sweet little panda charms on them. One says BEST and the other says FRIENDS. Because that's what we are.

When you put the two charms together they look like this.

Matilda came over while I was showing Ava and Daisy. So I asked her if she wanted to see my necklace too.

When Matilda saw the little panda her eyes went really big!

She said, "It's . . . um . . . really pretty."

Then she gave me a big smile. A secret kind of smile.

I wonder why she did that?

☺livia

After school

I just went over to visit our new neighbors again. Nobody was home. 😞 But guess what I discovered when I came back to my room?

The tape on my room-enterer detector was broken!

And so was the string!!

Someone has been in my ROOM! AGAIN!!!

I just don't know who. 😕

I need to invent a new, even better
invention so I will know who the room-
enterer is.

☺livia

Wonderful Wednesday

When I got home from school, Mom said there was a surprise for me in her study.

And guess what it was?

Not the **real** Lucy—Lucy's head, on Mom's computer. And she was wearing her necklace with the FRIENDS charm on it.

Phew. I guess that means she still thinks I'm her best friend. ☺

We talked and talked and talked. She told me all about her new house. And her new school. And the new friends she's made.

And I told her all about my new bedroom.
And Donkey. And the new girl in our class.

Lucy wanted to know everything about
her.

So many questions! And I hardly knew the answers to any of them. Maybe I should get to know Matilda better so I can find out!

☺livia

Super Invention Thursday

Ava and Daisy came over after school to see my new room. I asked Matilda too, but she said she had to help her mom with something. ☹

It was the perfect time to test out my latest invention. It's called the Super-Duper Drink and Snack Fetcher!

I made it last night. I had to borrow a few extra parts for it from around the house.

Hey! What happened to the mop? And where's the bucket?

Mo-omm! Olivia's Been IN MY Room aGain!!!

ELLA'S BiG Box of CRAFT STUFF!

Here's what it looks like.

SPECIAL
pulling Gadget

Bit OF OLD
broomstick

STAIRS

Bucket FOR
SNACKS

ROPE

Helpful Little BROTHER
to Get snacks from the
Kitchen and put them in the
Bucket for YOU

Ava and Daisy sat up in my room, waiting hungrily for the snacks to arrive. I pulled up the bucket with the special pulling gadget.

It's called a pulley! ☺

And guess what?

Max didn't put snacks in the bucket.

He put <u>SLUGS</u> from OUR garden in instead.

Big, slippery, slimy ones!

Olivia

Skipping-song Friday

Ava and Daisy and Sage and Samira and I were skipping rope at lunchtime.

Sage and Samira were twirling the big jump rope. And Ava and Daisy and I were taking turns running in and out, singing our skipping song.

Ice cream SUNDAE
CHERRY ON TOP,
Who's YOUR BEST friend?
I FORGOT!

And then you skip on the spot and call out the letters of the alphabet. If you trip on the rope you're out. And you have to say the name of someone starting with the last letter you said.

And guess which letter I went out on?

 For Lucy.

My best friend forever. I really, really, really wish she didn't have to go away. ☹

Then I saw Matilda watching us play. So I whispered to Ava, "We should ask Matilda to play too."

And Ava whispered back, "Sure."

So we did. And Matilda was a really, really, really good skipper! She knew some cool skipping songs too.

Like this one.

Chim-a-roo cheetahs
Turn around
Chim-a-roo cheetahs
Touch the ground
Chim-a-roo cheetahs
Show your spots
Chim-a-roo cheetahs

HOT, HOT, hot!

☺livia

~~Saturday~~ Spiderday

Here are the special secret plans for my new, improved invention. This will help me catch the mystery room-enterer for sure!

NEW IMPROVED

Room-enterer Detector

FAKE spider

CHewed chewing GUM

string

I secretly borrowed this from Max's plastic bug collection. I hope he doesn't notice it's missing!

Door frame

DOOR

Dad's old video camera

One hour later 🕐

Guess what?

I tried out my new invention. And it worked! You **won't believe** who it was!

Oops!

☺livia

Wombat Sunday?

Something very strange is going on in Benny and Ollie's backyard. It looks like a ginormous wombat, digging a hole.

I'm just going to get my special super-magnifying binoculars so I can see it better.

A **bit** later --

OOOOOOOOOOO! It's not a wombat.
It's MATILDA!

She must be Benny and Ollie's big sister!

Now she's stopped digging the first hole
and has started another one. I wonder
what she's looking for?

Book Nook Monday

Ava and Daisy and
Sage and Samira
and I were sitting
on our special
cushions in the
Book Nook today.

I was just about to tell them all about
what I saw last night. And then suddenly
Matilda was right there! In the library! She
was reading a joke book and giggling quietly
with Jamila and Hannah G. So I waved to
her and she came in and sat down.

Next to me.

On *Lucy's* cushion.
☹☹☹

I guess she didn't **know** it was Lucy's cushion. She doesn't even know who Lucy *is*.

But it still made me a bit sad. ☹

Anyway, I was **busting** to know why Matilda was acting like a wombat in her backyard last night.

So I asked her.

And she said, "That wasn't me. I wasn't even there."

But her face went all red when she was saying it. Just like the tomatoes on Lucy's cushion.

☹livia

Monday, after dinner 🍴

I just heard a scream! So I looked out my window and guess who I saw?

Matilda! She was
playing pirates in
the playhouse
with Benny and
Ollie. With pirate

swords! And a gangplank! And a flag!

And the boys were making Matilda walk
the plank. It looked really fun! Ella never
wants to do stuff like that.

When her brothers ran back inside, Matilda
started digging holes again. Under the big
tree in the corner this time.

Maybe she's looking for buried treasure? Like a real pirate!

Or trying to dig down to the middle of the Earth?

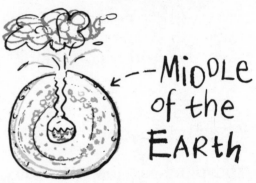

← - - MioᴼLe of the EARth

Or maybe her dad makes soggy tomato sandwiches every day for her to take to school. And she's burying them in the backyard so she won't get into trouble for not eating them.

I hate soggy sandwiches! I never, ever eat them. Last year I left some in my lunchbox. And then I forgot to take my lunchbox out of my bag. And it was Easter vacation. So they were stuck inside my bag for *two whole weeks*.

And this happened.

EWW!

It's OK, Dad. It's for my science experiment at school. They're supposed to look like that!

I'm going to ask Matilda all about what she was doing tomorrow. Pinkie swear!

☺livia

Troublesome Tuesday

I asked Matilda why she was digging holes in her backyard as soon as I got to school. And she just tossed her head and said, "I don't know what you're talking about."

So I told her I saw her out in her backyard last night. Under the tree.

And she said that must have been when she was taking her dog outside.

Matilda doesn't even have a dog.

So why would she tell me she did?

Have to go now. It's time for soccer practice in the park!

☺livia

Partner-hunt Wednesday

Today in gym Mr. Platt said we had to find a partner for a ball game. But all my friends were already paired up.

Except for Matilda.

Matilda   Sage   Samira   Ava   Daisy

I didn't want a partner who tells fibs. But I didn't want to be on my own either. And Matilda looks fun to be around sometimes. So I waved at her to come over.

Jamila   Ivy   ME

But Matilda pretended not to see me. Then she ran over to the boys and made a pair with Jonno. She can do really good traps and kicks. And run really fast. Faster than everyone else in the class!

If Matilda was my friend, I'd ask her if she wanted to join my soccer team.

But sometimes she goes all weird when I try to talk to her. She's not like that with anyone else. Maybe she just doesn't want to be friends with me.

☹livia

Matilda is out in her backyard again!
I can see her through
my binoculars.

This time she is
digging holes behind
the playhouse. And
guess who is curling
around her feet?

DoNKey!

I've started his detective cat training. He didn't like learning how to sit much.

So I taught him how to send me messages by swishing his tail instead.

SiT!

1   One Swish   = yes

2   Two Swishes   = NO

3   Three Swishes = Maybe

4   Four Swishes   = DANGER!

BEWARE!
RUN AWAY!

Now Donkey must be doing close-up spying on Matilda for me! I can't wait to see what he finds out!

☺livia

Bad News Thursday

I couldn't understand Donkey's messages last night. His tail was too twitchy to count the swishes properly. And then he went off chasing mice.

I don't think he is going to be a very good detective cat after all. 😵

Now I'm never going to find out what Matilda is doing.

😞livia

Friendship Friday

The most amazing thing happened at school today!

I was just hanging up my backpack outside our classroom when someone softly tapped my arm. And guess who it was?

Matilda!

She said she had to show me something really important that she found last night.

Yes! The **important thing** must have been in one of the holes! I couldn't **wait** to find out what it was!

But first Matilda showed me something else. A message from Lucy!

Dear New Girl,

I hope you like sleeping in my old room.
I am really going to miss it! But I am
going to miss my friend Olivia even more.

Olivia lives in the house on the other side
of the back fence. She and I have been
BFFs 4 ever.

I would like you to be Olivia's new BFF
so she won't be sad when I move away.

But first of all you have to pass my
secret challenge! ⟶

☆ ❊ SECRET CHALLENGE ☆
♡

I have hidden a new pair of
friendship charms somewhere in our
backyard. If you can find them, it
will prove you are a true friend.

You must keep one of the charms
yourself, and give the other half to
Olivia. And then you have to promise
to be her new BFF 4 ever. (Cross
your heart hope to die.)

Love,
Lucy

Matilda found Lucy's note in her closet on the very first night in her new house.

So now I know why Matilda kept staring at me when I was telling our class what I could see from my new room. And when I was showing my friends my new necklace.

She wanted to know which girl at school was me!

And most importantly, I now know why she was digging all those holes! ☺

Then Matilda showed me the important thing.

The charms that Lucy buried in her backyard. She did find them! She passed the secret challenge! I can't wait to tell Lucy next time we chat! ☺ ☺ ☺

And then Matilda told me something really, really icky. There was something else in the hole. Right next to the charms.

A dead mouse. With some of its guts on the outside.

Icky

Donkey must have buried it in there. Just like Bob does with his slobbery old bones. Maybe Donkey is a good detective cat after all. He was helping Matilda find the charms!

"Eww!" we both said. At exactly the same time. "Disgusting!"

And then we laughed and laughed until we both got ginormous stitches in our tummies.

I have to go now. Matilda is going to show me the hole where she found Lucy's charms.

And I'm going to show her my plans for my super-duper birthday playhouse.

And then we're going to go to the park to play soccer.

Do you want to know the best thing?

It's Friday! Which means we've got the whole weekend to play together!

livia